Dear Alex and Seamus,
Merry Christmass!
2002
Love,
Jenny

Animals sleep in the stable and barn.
Snowflakes are falling on Paradise Farm . . .

For David
Birdsong

First U.S. edition 2002

Library of Congress Cataloging-in-Publication Data

Ashforth, Camilla.
Willow at Christmas / Camilla Ashforth.
p.   cm.
Summary: Willow and Little Pig Pink prepare to celebrate Christmas with their friends and the animals on Paradise Farm.
ISBN 0-7636-1850-0
[1. Teddy bears—Fiction. 2. Christmas—Fiction. 3. Farm life—Fiction.] I. Title.
PZ7.A823 We 2002
[E]—dc21   2001043759

Printed in Italy

2 4 6 8 10 9 7 5 3 1

This book was typeset in Columbus.
The illustrations were done in watercolor and pencil.

Candlewick Press
2067 Massachusetts Avenue
Cambridge, Massachusetts 02140

visit us at www.candlewick.com

WILLOW

at Christmas

Camilla Ashforth

CANDLEWICK PRESS
CAMBRIDGE, MASSACHUSETTS

Willow loves the crisp cold days
and cozy nights of Christmas.

For weeks he watches from Paradise Farm
for a sign of the first snow of winter.

PARADISE FARM

At last, one morning, Willow woke to whiteness.
The snow had come in the night.

"Hooray!" cried Willow. He jumped out of bed.
"Snow on Christmas Eve!"

He pulled on his clothes, his coat, and his boots
and went to find Little Pig Pink.

They walked the horse around the yard.

They broke the ice on the water trough.

They led the sheep to a sheltered field

and brought fresh straw for the hens.

On their way back home for breakfast,
Willow picked armfuls of holly.

At home he found a card on the mat.
Merry Christmas
Love, your friend Finley

"I do hope Finley comes over later,"
said Willow at breakfast.

He sat beside Little Pig Pink
at the fire, making toast and
planning their Christmas.

They had presents
to wrap for the
animals. Willow
wrote the tags.

Together they baked
a Christmas cake.
Little Pig Pink
licked the bowl.

They tied the holly
on long red ribbons
and hung it from
the beams.

"Now all we need
is the Christmas tree,"
said Willow to
Little Pig Pink.

Willow collected a spade and a sack
and they set out for Yanwath Wood.

Over the fields, up on the hill,
Through the snowy winter chill,
There's a forest of fairy-tale charm.
We'll find a tree there for Paradise Farm.
It's Christmas day in the morning.
It's Christmas day in the morn.

YANWATH WOOD

They searched the woods for the perfect tree.

"This is too tall. That one's too thin . . .

and this is far too tiny."

"Here's the one!" cried Willow at last.

"The prettiest tree in the wood."

Little Pig Pink and Willow carried it carefully home.

That evening, as they hung the tree with little bells
and baubles, they heard the sound of cheerful
voices singing Christmas carols.

Outside the snow was falling hard.
"Merry Christmas! Come on in!"
said Willow to his friends.

Wish, Finley, and Long Tom joined Willow

and Little Pig Pink, to celebrate Christmas

and friendship by the fire at Paradise Farm.

Later Willow set out
with Little Pig Pink
to deliver the
animals' presents.

"Merry Christmas,
horse," said Willow.

"Merry
Christmas,
hens.

"Merry Christmas,
  cows . . .
    and geese.

"And sweet
  Christmas dreams
  to you all."

"You can stay with me tonight,"
said Willow to Little Pig Pink.

"We'll hang our stockings at the foot
of the bed and wait for Santa Claus."

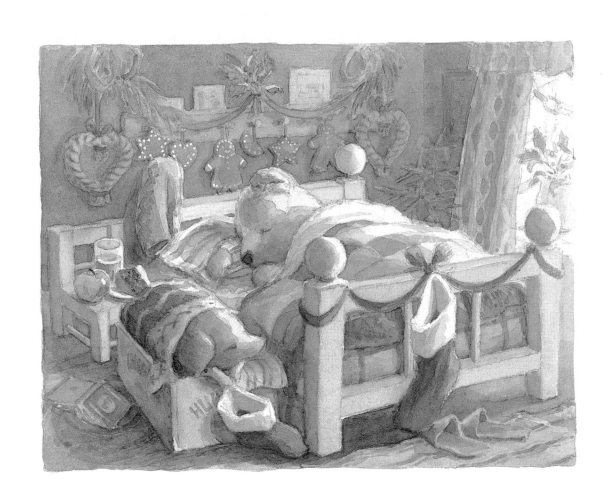

They snuggled down in their cozy beds.
Their eyes began to close.

Paradise Fields on Christmas night,
All is still, all is white.
Animals sleep in the stable and barn.
Snowflakes are falling on Paradise Farm.
White Christmas wishes for all.
White Christmas wishes for all.

It was well before dawn when Willow woke.
"Little Pig Pink!" he whispered. "I think
Santa Claus has come."

They reached for their stockings
and spilled them out.

First Little Pig Pink found chocolate truffles,
an apple, and marzipan eggs. Willow unwrapped
a wind-up hen, a whistle, and a wobbly duck.

Little Pig Pink found a patchwork rug
and Willow, a cozy red jacket.

As dawn broke on Paradise Farm, the animals gathered round, all dressed up in their brand-new presents.

Merry Christmas,
Willow and Little Pig Pink!
MERRY CHRISTMAS, EVERYONE!

Willow's Christmas Song